THE MEMORIES OF LONDON TAXI DRIVER

Author A. CAN

Table of Contents

First Day at Work: The Beginning of Night Shifts

My mobile app chimed. I felt satisfied because I got my first customer. After two long years of hard work, this moment felt important. My heart raced with nervous excitement as I watched the little car icon move closer to the pickup spot. I lead a fairly normal life, working most days as an engineer. Countless calculations and technical drawings fill my workdays, and they pay the bills. But recently, I took on a side hassle as a taxi driver. It felt like a great match. The hours are flexible, I get paid daily, and best of all, I can interact with people without the stress of bartending. So how has it been? Let me tell you. I arrived at a polished office building to meet a woman who was standing outside. Her—was it a blazer? I couldn't tell at first. She had her phone in one hand and was draped over one arm. When I confirmed her identity, she looked up and smiled. Yes, it was Claire. I met her with a smile and a friendly sidestep, inviting her into the back seat of my car.

"Did you have a long day?" I inquired, steering away from the edge of the street.

"The longest," she replied, her accent carrying hints of the North. Yorkshire, perhaps.
"Board meetings always drain the life out of me. I'm ready to kick off these torture devices."
She pointed to her elegant heels with a laugh. She had a way of lowering defences right away. She was professional but not pretentious. As we drove through evening traffic, our chat flowed easily. We talked about the weather, which was unseasonably warm. Then, she mentioned her favourite takeout spot—a Thai place I need to try. Finally, we discussed her work in marketing. It's tough, but she finds it rewarding.

"And what about you?" she asked, leaning slightly forward. "Is driving your main job?"
I saw her eyes in the rearview mirror—warm brown with flecks of amber catching the setting sunlight. For a brief moment, I felt a flip of attraction—that rusty sensation I hadn't allowed myself to feel in ages.
"No, I'm an engineer," I said, deftly manoeuvring past a double-parked delivery van. "Mostly, I work freelance. This is just to even out the financial bumps."
"Clever," she said, with the appreciation of an unrestrained applause. "This is the hassle economy at its finest."
As we approach her destination, she was tidying up and preparing to leave when she stopped and hit me with this bombshell.

"You know, if I had more drivers like you, I'd take cars instead of the Tube more often," she said, smiling with her eyes.

When she departed, I lingered for a moment, letting the experience sink in. If every rider is going to be this charming, I mused, this work will be tremendous. At lease that is what I thought!!

Gold Digger of the Night

I picked up a couple outside a fancy nightclub in the city. A young man dressed sharply, and a woman looked like she had come off a magazine cover. Her smile was impressive but looked a little too practiced and used for my taste. I know the type. I've met a few. And I know all the moves they make. I'll admit I was feeling a bit negative about it. I often do it when things feel the same with no real change. When they got into my backseat, his cologne mixed with her perfume. The scent filled the front of the car, creating a captivating cloud. As he told me his address, his eyes remained glued to her. I saw their faces in the rearview mirror. He looked dreamy and hopeful. She had a practiced, almost enchanted way about her. The young man with the starry eyes was totally lost inside a come-on, while she kept coming back to her phone. Something electric and personal was happening back there. Halfway to where we were headed, her phone brightened. She took the call as if it were the most normal thing in the world.

She said, "Hi Elaine," and her voice softened. "Yeah, I met a nice man, and I'm going to be late."

The voice at the other end interrupted her. I couldn't make out what was being said, but the whole thing was impeccable.

"Oh my God," she breathed, protecting her heart with a hand. "What about her? Is she all right? Tell me now so I can get there soon."
The face of the young man immediately fell. "What is wrong?"

"My mother is quite ill," she said, with eyes full of false sympathy. "Can we meet some other time? I'm so sorry, but I have to take care of her right now."
His disappointment was real enough, but he bounced back quickly. He wanted to be her hero.
"What's wrong? How can I help?"
"I need to call another taxi to bring me back to my house," she stated, and was already making for her phone. "It is imperative that I arrive there as soon as possible."
"No, no," he explained, nudging forward to capture my attention in the rear-view mirror. "Driver, might we alter our current course? Let us take her back to her house first." " Sure, just changed the destination on the app " I said.
I watched as he put a soft hand on hers. His warm gesture made knowing what was about to happen seem so much more awful.

"Don't worry, sweetheart," he said, his voice full of the kind of caring that warms a mother's heart.

"She'll pull through fine. Just get to her and be the great daughter I'm sure you are to her. If you run into trouble, don't hesitate to call me. I'm here for you."

I stopped so he could get out and find another ride to his place. As I was about to shut the door, he gave me a serious look I wasn't quite expecting. "Take care of her!" he said, and then the door was closed. "Of course," I said, a knot of tension forming in my stomach as I pulled away. After he left, I saw her change in the mirror. The look of concern vanished, replaced by a self-satisfied grin as she took out her phone once more.

"Yeah, he just left," she laughed into the receiver, kicking off her heels and stretching across the backseat like a satisfied cat.

"Oh yeah, he paid for everything—food, drinks, even my taxi. What dumbass. He actually thought I was going to sleep with him!"

"It always works, sweetheart. You know that. Don't worry; it's your turn next. Next time you're out, I will certainly repay the favour. Count on it, darling."

Her laughter was still ringing off the car walls as I twisted to look at her. She talked like I wasn't there, like I was just part of the vehicle—not a person with ears to hear or a mind to judge. In her world, it was as if drivers were invisible or too insignificant to matter. Once I had dropped her off at the corner next to her apartment building, I sat in my car for several seconds. Our dispatch system includes a messaging feature that passengers can use to contact us. I knew it was wrong, but I also knew I was going to do it anyway: I was going to message him and ask him to call me. I did tell him everything I heard when he called me back. A long silence filled the other end for a time.

"What is your reason for telling me this?" he at last queried, his tone flat.

I confessed, *"My ex did the exact same thing to me. She cleaned out my bank account before she left. I didn't want you to go through the same thing."*

A lengthy silence. "I appreciate it," he said before terminating the call. As I directed my taxi back into the fray of highway traffic, I wondered if I had done the right thing. Sometimes, keeping someone safe from fake love and heartbreak is the kindest thing you can do.

Young Gay Couple

It was a Sunday morning at 3 AM two young gay couples; they are university students. The two men looked happy after spending a night in London while showing signs of being too drunk. I have built my reputation by treating all my taxi riders with friendship through casual conversations that create enjoyable trips. Before starting the ride to their drop-off point, I checked their destination through the app. Since the account holder appeared intoxicated, I provided him some helpful suggestions. I informed the passenger through the rearview mirror that he should notify me if he becomes unwell so I could stop the vehicle somewhere safe then you would not puke in my taxi.

He mumbled those words before resting his weight against the window. The account holder sat quietly until drop off point of our trip, but his speaking partner kept up a conversation with me. he shared with me details about their academic life and their evening out while expressing positive thoughts about their experience in London. The conversation between us had a positive tone, which occasionally became interesting. Soon after reaching out our destination point, the expected event occurred. The passenger who used his account became ill while seated behind me in my taxi. He vomit, after the incident that I remained calm since people often vomit after heavy drinking.

Since they were students and the students' budget constraints directed my attempt to provide them an economical solution. There was A professional car cleaning service operates 24 hours per day. The car cleaning would most likely cost fifty British pounds. The money you need to pay through the app amounts to approximately 100 pounds because it covers both the cleaning expenses and my waiting time. The account holder stared at me while his body swayed gently then he said ten pounds would be sufficient to cover the expense.

Obviously, the amount of money offered was not enough to cover cleaning and my waiting time. So, I told them that I would follow normal procedure and report it through the application system. I wished them good night before they left the car. I drove to the 24-hour car wash, where I captured evidence photos of the damage before submitting the report to the app together with my payment receipt. The app eventually delivered the regular cleaning fee of 100 pounds about sixty minutes after the submission. After completing my duties by finishing the taxi cleaning, I went home unaware that the incident would affect my work.

I tried to access my account on the following day but discovered that customer service from the app had blocked my account. I became puzzled, so I reached out to their support team by phone. The representative stated that my account received a suspension because of an intense complaint. A client reported about using discriminatory language while driving him during the last night. "What?" I exclaimed, genuinely shocked. I make it a point to never express such words to anyone.

I presented my version of events to the representative while being honest, but he did not show any sign of sympathy. The complaint about you remains extremely serious. The system stands inactive until all matters get finalized. The customer service declined to provide their details because their privacy policies were in effect. According to the representative, they needed a court order to share that information.

My frustration led to legal action after I knew my innocence because I refused to accept the false accusation. I took the necessary steps by filing an online complaint, followed by legal procedures to prove my innocence. After the court issued its summons, the company was obligated to hand over the passenger details. The police station in North London ordered all of us to give statements after the incident. When I arrived for the interview, there were three young men instead of two entering the building. The additional person they added to their case turned out to be a fake witness who joined the other two to back their claim.

The officer who talked with me took his work seriously. "This is a serious accusation. You should weigh the decision to move forward with this case. Having no evidence of your innocence could lead to getting a criminal record. My smile confused him as he tried to understand my reaction. Then suddenly, "Don't tell me you had CCTV in your Taxi", he said with a sure smile. His gaze shifted from me to the recording evidence he just discovered. His expression shifted when he asked if I possessed evidence. "I do," I confirmed. "Twenty-three minutes and forty-five seconds of the entire journey."

He requested to watch the recorded evidence right away. He finished watching the footage and returned to the interview rooms before speaking to every participant. And, he called them in our interview room. As soon as the young men entered the room, my presence made them restless. The officer silenced them firmly. He spoke directly to them, announcing his final opportunity to receive truthful information.

"I give you one chance to come clean "he said.

They never changed their position that I had treated them unfairly. The officer lost his patience then

"I just watched a movie, and you were starring in it"

said and he press play and started video footage, showed the complete journey. The officer told his fake witness that he did not appear together on camera but were now making conflicting statements. The suspects stuck to their lies before hearing the evidence recording. He confessed to the officer that he did not plan to take part in the activity. They promised me everything would be safe, and I could earn a lot from the deal. I'm sorry, and start crying. The officers displayed their strong emotional reaction, especially because these young men had successfully misled them during their interviews. During the whole ride, I acted with respect and respectfulness, which the video confirmed.

The lead officer spoke to me privately. The officers believe you are not guilty and stand ready to back your decision to file official charges. These students lack awareness that taking such action will put their job prospects at risk. A father like yourself knows best what to do with this situation. While staying innocent, I chose to let the case end if they issued an official confession of their wrongdoing and a signed document to shield me from future legal actions.

They quickly consented because they wanted to escape criminal prosecution. I received a message from the app company after the passenger sent his admission of lying. About 10 minutes later I received message from the app

"Our team regrets the problem and has enabled your account with a £500 credit to make up for the trouble you had."

I finished my work that day with both parties free from prosecution while holding their written admissions. They maintained their apologies while moving away. This encounter demonstrated that individuals who misuse their identity for money will get exposed to the truth. Keeping honest records while showing patience through documented evidence shields you from false accusations.

Driver with an accusation of sexual assault.

I reached the chicken shop in Enfield at 4 AM to place my order. Only one or two customers remained in the store since most people had gone home earlier. I began talking with the business owner, who had droopy eyes but a friendly smile, while I waited for my food. The topic shifted to what he did before this moment. For fifteen years he worked as a taxi driver until he decided to share this information while cleaning the counter. *"I will always stay away from that work, never."* He said.

His tone caught my attention. As a Taxi drive myself, I was immediately curious. After learning about my book project, he welcomed me to sit down as he prepared to shut the shop. He uttered a combination of surrender and joy while showing he wanted to tell me his tale. He started sharing his story by taking his seat at the table. *"The job enabled me to pay expenses and support my family. I had a wife, children, and regular family life."* He said.

"Had?" The response caught my attention when he talked about times that had passed. He smiled carefully.

"I will tell you the whole bloody story."
He revealed that weekend night shifts brought most of his income because although dealing with drunk passengers was hard sometimes the reward was enough to keep doing them. The night that altered everything appeared.
During that night, I transported a young female passenger. The woman appeared to be incredibly drunk since she struggled to stand upright. I ended our drive at her drop-off location and came outside to assist her because she could not walk. His gaze shifted to the distance while he thought back. He helped her get out of the car by opening the door and supported her as she struggled to stand. Before leaving, she fell unexpectedly.
He showed her the position of her fall by using his hands to show that he head pitched toward the curb.
"It was instinct, you know? I jumped ahead and held her body steady by taking her shoulders and protecting her head. The curb edge, formed by concrete and metal, made a dangerous point. If her head had hit that... she could have died or injured seriously" he said.
She shouted repeatedly, "Leave me alone," while he tried to assist her. I told her why I grabbed her, but she refused to listen. He ended the conversation because the drunk passenger resisted his help, so he drove home without thinking about it.

He went on but needed a moment to compose himself before adding, "Police officers showed up at my home the following day. The police arrested me in front of my entire family, including my wife and children, for sexual assault of a female rider. His voice wavered slightly. "The shame of it... and the look on my wife's face. That's what still haunts me. She stared at me with a judgmental expression before anyone said anything. The store's heat failed to protect me from the cold feeling that crossed my skin. He stared at me without blinking because there was nothing he needed to conceal.

He spoke in a low voice about his sixteen years as a married man. I shared my bed and life with my wife for sixteen whole years. I never once cheated on her. During that instant when I required her faith the most... He shook his head. The neighbours observed from their house windows as officers arrested him. He told his story to police at the station, but they had only his version because the passenger denied their encounter. He proposed looking for security cameras, but police told him no cameras existed in that area, but the existing ones doesn't cover that spot where you drop her off. The authorities placed me in a detention area for their inquiry. Days turned into weeks. Weeks into months. After three months in detention, he recalled this experience. As my wife sent the divorce documents without discussion, she filed for separation. Just sent the papers to sign. She obtained child custody rights and misled our children about me to the children. The lifestyle I had before vanished completely when I attempted to assist and save someone. *"How did you get out?"* My thoughts focused on his answer while I stopped eating my meal.

His expression softened slightly. My brother stayed loyal to me throughout. He kept checking that area to find any useful information. One day, as his attempt at finding work failed, he stood outside a barbershop and observed the security camera in inside of their display window. The store owner verified that the recording was active even though the camera pointed toward from the inside of the shop to outside. The security camera happened to point to the spot where the incident occurred, and its system had not reached the cycle limit of deleting older videos yet.

My brother's determination saved me. Otherwise, my freedom would have ended if he had arrived at the scene after the three-day period. He did not need to complete his sentence. The video displayed the events precisely as I described them. She slipped, and I reached her in time to prevent her from falling onto the curb. Clear as day. His brother gave his lawyer the evidence, which included both the video and the barber's testimony. He was released immediately.

"During my three months of detention, I suffered complete loss of life. My family, my job, my reputation. He cleaned his palms across each other to erase the incident from his mind. The charges I filed against her for lying turned out to be ineffective since she blamed her alcohol consumption for misunderstanding what happened. Got away with just a fine. Never spent a day inside."

He gained money back from his wrongful imprisonment, and together with his brother's help, he bought this chicken shop. According to him, he purchased his home and established his business, which made his ex-wife want to rejoin him. "I refused," he said. Things that work out for the better often stem from negative beginnings. Following sixteen years as a taxi driver brought me no rewards except a wife who did not appreciate me. I acquired this business and minimized my work hours to save money while revealing in my life.

I shook my head. "That's quite a story, mate." He agreed with me and added that the lesson is to keep a camera in your vehicle all the time. Having this tool in your car will help keep you safe during dangerous moments. Next morning, after my promise, I installed a camera system inside my Taxi. His experience demonstrated that taking simple safety measures can stop disastrous events from happening. During my drive that day, I realized our built life can vanish rapidly while finding true worth requires us to lose everything first.

Young Teenager Strip Show

I installed a taxi camera immediately when the chicken shop owner shared his cautionary experience. The story he told struck me because life collapses rapidly when there is no proof to validate reality. I took this basic protective measure unaware that it would serve me well in the near future. The incident took place during late Friday evening hours, which turned into early Saturday daylight. A woman in her late teenage or early twenties became my passenger when I collected her from Central London. The young woman took her place in the back seat while I drove through night traffic toward her final stop. A mysterious sound stopped me when I got close to Brixton Junction and made the left turn onto a side street. My eyes moved to the mirror, where I encountered something shocking. The young woman continued to mutter nonsense while she actually took off her clothing.

I broke into the short exclamation of disbelief before stopping my car at by the curb. My heartbeat raced while I turned off the engine and took my keys before exiting the taxi. My years of driving experience had never led me to this type of encounter before. The situation terrified me because of the similar incident involving the chicken shop owner. The situation forced me to move out of the car because remaining there would be too dangerous. My hands shook uncontrollably while I reached for the phone to dial 999. I stood at a secure distance from my car while leaning against a low wall until the police officers came. My skin felt cold and clammy as I stood under the unusual nighttime air temperature.

"Are you alright, mate?"

The voice startled me. A woman of about thirty approached me while her eyes focused on the streetlight. Something comfortable emerged from her facial expression. I forced a response through my unsteady voice that matched my fragile state. *"What's happening?"* she asked, stepping closer. You should breathe deeply, then talk at a controlled pace. I took a deep breath because she ordered me to do so. So, I introduced myself to the woman as a taxi driver. The passenger inside the taxi began removing her clothes after we left. The situation forced me out of the vehicle because I could not remain inside. I've called the police. She faced my taxi and inspected the passenger through the window glass while she seated in the back. Her expression showed confirmation of what I had described to her.

"Did you call the police?" She faced me again to inquire about the situation.

"Yes, they're on their way." I ran a hand through my hair. *"My God, what a nightmare."* She said this to me while giving a comforting smile. *"Got a cigarette?"* I reached into my pocket to get my cigarettes while nodding at her request. I extended the cigarette to her as I continued to tremble from shock. She recommended waiting with a cigarette while she maintained her cool and steady tone.

"I'll be your witness. I'll help you out." For the first time, I looked at her face and saw her warm brown eyes, kind smile, and confident composure, which seemed divine at that instant. A gentle beam from the streetlamp illuminated her figure, which made me experience a feeling that seemed closer to something stronger than mere gratitude.

"Thank you," I said sincerely. *"I really appreciate it."* She tried to make the moment less stressful through casual talk. She presented herself as Julia, then revealed that she worked as a bartender in the area before going home from work. She stood out with her entire being, including her looks and her willingness to assist a stranger without delay. A female officer joined us after the police arrived. *"Who called this in?"* she asked. I moved ahead to speak. After seeing my taxi, the officer returned her attention to me with a sceptical expression.

"What did you do?" she asked, her tone accusatory.

I was stunned into silence. Despite my proper actions, she started by blaming me for the trouble. As I remained speechless, Julia took a stand between us, showing strong anger. The police officer sounds perplexed when she asks this unusual inquiry. She demanded, her voice rising. The man left his car to park at this spot. His hands were shaking! He's the one who called you! The moment the officer saw me, she wanted to know what I had done. She pointed vigorously toward my taxi. You must see the young lady is under the influence of drugs and alcohol. She is too intoxicated and disoriented to make sound decisions. The man emerged from his own vehicle to call you.

The officer took a step back. "I didn't mean—" Julia interrupted to say,

"You should request the right information first." "That's your duty."

While Julia fought aggressively to protect me like an advocate, she helped me recover my composure. I retrieved my words to tell her that I have a vehicle camera. The young woman's actions and my corresponding, appropriate response were plainly evident in the video the police viewed. They tried to talk to her and put something to cover her body. After about forty minutes, they said that they would like for me to take her the rest of the way to her home.

"No," I stated with confidence. *"Absolutely not. If I couldn't establish my innocence when you first came to me, then how in the world could I do so now at drop off point to her relatives, just as things are getting more intense? I don't feel safe, and I shouldn't feel unsafe. Take her out of my car. This isn't happening anymore."*

Another half hour had to go by before they got her out of my car and into the ambulance. She was, as I had suspected, under the influence of alcohol and drugs. They took our details and finally cleared us to leave.

"I will take you home," I said to Julia after the officers left.

"I was merely acting the way anyone should act," she said, a modest smile on her face. And somehow that smile made the whole street brighter. Upon our arrival at her place, she extended an invitation for coffee. At first, I declined, but her insistence and the kindness in her eyes rendered me unable to refuse. Her apartment was cozy, yet compact. I told her my chicken shop story.

"You saved yourself a lot of trouble with that decision," she said. *"And maybe that man's story happened just so you'd be prepared for tonight."*

Her presence was magnetic, a natural warmth that put me at ease, even in the chaos of the evening. When it came time to leave, I thanked her again and offered my services whenever she might need a ride.

"I should really get home to my wife and kids," I said at last, though a part of me was reluctant to end our conversation.

I was driving home, remembering the chicken shop owner's experience with his wife, and decided to do a little test. When I got home, I told my wife about the incident. I left out any mention of Julia or the camera footage. Her response filled me with joy.

"I trust you," she said, while I hesitated. *"I've known you for one-third of my life. You've always been anything but lazy and have devoted your life to our kids. I have no doubts about you."*

It was only then that I brought up the camera and my witness. She smiled as if she knew something.

"Are you trying to find out how far I can be pushed?"

She asked, with a look that saw me for what I really was. We laughed together, and she added, *"It's a good thing you put the camera in your car."*

That night, as I reclined on my pillow, considering the day's events, I thought about how differently things might have turned out without the camera—or without Julia's surprise intervention. You never know when an angel might show up, in forms you never expect. Existence has a way of instructing us to be ready for that which is unanticipated. But it also instructs us that, even in our shadowy moments, there are virtuous souls willing to stand shoulder to shoulder with us—shining beacons of humanity, arriving at our side just when we could use their presence the most.

Saving a Drunken Woman on Christmas Nights

It was Christmas night, and I was quite busy. Prices were twice higher, and I was making good money. I was fortunate that there was a young couple who needed a trip for a long distance—Central, almost to the M25 border. My quoted fare was excellent. They got into my taxi, and I set off. She was quite obviously drunk and out of control. I knew it instantly. I locked my doors on my side for safety in case she opened them while we were moving. I was nearly there, traveling on a dual carriageway, when this young man signalled for me to pull in.

"*I really need to piss,*" he exclaimed urgently.

"*I can't stop on this dual carriageway,*" I told him.

"*Let me take the next exit and pull in somewhere safe.*"

"*Okay,*" he said.

I pulled over as soon as I could and was able to get just enough space to pull the taxi to the side of the road with some bushes in front of it a short distance away. I opened both doors and the young man walked to the bushes to urinate. In his absence, I heard a click. I knew instantly that she was trying to get out. I opened my door as fast as I could, but she was already walking out and into oncoming traffic in a state of inebriation without knowing the hazard. His companion saw what was happening and tried to pull his own trousers up and urinated on himself, rushing to get back. There was no time to waste. I made a run through the stream of racing cars and scooped her up behind me—she was terribly thin and light. I pulled her to safety on the curb just as a car whizzed past.

"Let go of me! Let go of me!"
she was yelling without even realizing that she'd nearly killed herself as a car passed with high speed. If I'd been a couple of seconds late, she would've been dead. The young man quickened his pace toward me, his face ashen with terror and relief. His eyes met mine with a look of sheer appreciation.

"Thank you,"
He replied, his voice trembling.
"You risked your own life to save her. How can I ever repay you for that?"
"What is wrong with her?"
I wondered in amazement. She puffed a couple of times. She is stoned and doesn't know what she is doing," he said.

"I can see that,"
I said with adrenaline surging through my veins.

"Ghosh. Get her back to the taxi. I need a cigarette. I am stressed now."

"You deserve it," he said to me. "Sorry that you had to go through all this."
I took them to their address and waited while he took her in and put her safely to bed. When he returned outside, he instructed that I stay.
"Okay," I said. "I am done for the night; I will go straight home"
The young man escorted me to his kitchen and made coffee. I told him that I needed a cigarette, and he told me to let's go outside. As we sat outside to calm our nerves, he shook his head in wonder.

"I can't believe what just happened," he said. "You were like Superman, catching her just a moment before that oncoming car sped by. I couldn't get there in time. I don't know how to repay you."
He handed me £100.
"What is this for?" I asked.
"Go ahead and get yourself a decent dinner," he urged.
"No need," I replied.
"No, you really do deserve this."
The next day he told my company what I did. I was emailed thanking me for being a considerate person and with a bonus of a further £50 to my account. I didn't do it for reward—just what was right. She was in need; she was not herself. I almost got hit while trying to save her. Would I do it again? Yes. I

saved a young and inexperienced girl's life. I just hope that the next time she doesn't get stoned and drunk and walk on the highway.

Escape from Sex Slaver

I was waiting for passengers while on duty when another operator phoned. And told me he had passengers but no vehicles. It was a long-distance job for good pay, and I agreed to help. "In about five minutes," I told him because I was near their office.

"Are they your regular customers?" I asked.

"No, just passing passengers who asked for a taxi," he replied.

"OK, we need to get money up front," I insisted. They prepaid for my fare. There were two passengers: a man and a quite attractive young lady in her twenties. I sensed that there was something strange about them immediately, though I couldn't quite put my finger on what it was. They got into my taxi, and I set off to drive them to their destination about an hour away. During the course of the trip, I noticed that the woman was trying to say something, but the man seemed to be preventing her from speaking. After a while, the man suddenly said, "Can you stop by off-license? I need to get something." He assured me that he would not be long. Before he departed my taxi, he instructed me to

"wait there and keep her in. She doesn't know this place and might get scared. If anything goes wrong, just shout for me."

"Okay," I said.

The moment he emerged from the taxi, the woman whispered urgently,

"Save me."

"Repeat that again," I asked, not sure I'd heard it right.

"Save me," she pleaded with open eyes full of terror.

"Do you speak English?" I asked.

"No English, please save me," she whispered in a trembling voice.

"Where are you originally from?" I asked.

She mentioned a country in Eastern Europe, though I didn't catch what it was.

"The man took my phone," she went on in broken English.

Immediately, I used Phone app Voice Translator and asked her,

"What is wrong?"

It gave me a chill to my bones.

"I am a sex slave. He is a troublemaker. He has a knife."

I was surprised but did not hesitate.

"Get going before he comes back," she implored.

Without any delay, I left that man behind and drove off somewhere distant from that location where we would be able to discuss freely without any fears. Through my phone translator, she told me that she was coerced into prostitution and wanted to escape. He was threatening her.

"We should report this to the police," I said.

"No police," she exclaimed in alarm.

It was rare to see, but I was able to observe frustration and terror on her face. Her bright eyes were now covered with terror.

"Okay, what do you want me to do?" I asked.

"Please help me to go back my country," she pleaded. *"I do not want to stay here. He will find me."*

I didn't know what to do.

"You don't have a place to stay, do you?" I asked.

"No," she said softly.

Even to this day, I do not know whether what I did afterward was stupid or courageous. I called my wife and explained to her the whole thing and asked for her opinion.

"Bring her in," my wife ordered firmly. *"Let me talk to her and then we'll make a decision."*

Meanwhile, I called up the taxi office and told them what happened—without saying that I'd taken her home. I just said that I'd dropped her a mile away.

"Tell him that I was a one-off driver and that police were asking about him. If he is guilty, he'll run."

The operator called back later:

*"He came to ask about you, and after telling
him word for word what you said to me, he
took run off."*

Upon returning home, my wife conversed with
the young lady through the translator. After
about five minutes of dialogue, my wife came
out and said,

*"She is going to stay with us tonight and
tomorrow we are going to take her to the
airport and return her to her own country.
Simply get her a ticket."*

"Yes, boss," I replied with a smile.

I purchased her ticket and gave her about £200
pocket money. We took her to the airport the
day after and made sure she was on her flight
home. I asked my wife later why she was so
pleased to do it—most women would be
annoyed about having a total stranger stay.
Her reply was persuasive:

*"She can be our daughter too. What goes
around comes around."*

Seven days later, my wife was contacted by the
young lady using a friend to interpret. She told
her that she was deeply grateful for what we
did for her and invited us to visit her whenever
we went to her place. Four years later, post-
Covid, we went to Ukraine since it was on the
green list then. We bought our tickets from
Moldova since it was nearer to Odessa. We
went a couple of days prior and took four days

in Moldova to see her before returning to the UK.

This time she was speaking English—a blessed relief. She told us that she was a graduate of engineering school and was now a software engineer.

"All because of your help in helping save me," she said with tears of appreciation in her eyes. "I was young and stupid and fell into his trap. He made me work as a sex slave. By God's grace, you were my angels who saved me— both of you saved me."

She introduced us to her husband. She was with us each day for our four-day visit and took us around and introduced us to her family. She even took us to the airport to see us off with tears running down her face. My wife and I looked at each other and enjoyed the satisfaction of having saved not just a human life but also her future. She has two children now, and we take pride in having played a part in that. Some would question why I did not report to the police. When we travelled to see her in her native land, I wanted to know why she did not engage the police. "Police in my own country are corrupt," she said. "I thought it was everywhere." It was then that I understood why she was frightened. Had I been more compassionate towards her then, I would have been able to let her know that she would be fine with the police in England. However, I still

do not know why I acted as I did, but I am
thankful that I did.

Passenger Who Pu (shit) in the Taxi

I was driving around the city when something caught my eye. Another taxi driver had pulled over to the side of the road. He sat on the curb with his head buried between his hands, repeatedly slapping his own forehead. I pulled over and approached him, concerned. Most of us drivers help each other out—it's an unwritten rule of the profession.

"*Can I help?*" I asked, standing over him. He looked up at me, his eyes reflecting pure anguish.

"*This is a nightmare,*" he muttered. "*I'm just slapping my head to wake up from this nightmare.*"
His distress only deepened my curiosity.

"*What's happening, mate?*" I inquired.
"*Animals have more dignity than some who call themselves human,*" he replied cryptically, shaking his head.

I was struggling to piece together the situation. "*OK,*" I said, trying to remain calm.
"*Let's start again. What's happening?*"
"*Actually, he shits... pu* " he stammered, barely able to get the words out.
"*Who pu, shit?*" I asked, still confused.
"*Passenger,*" he replied flatly.

"What? Where?" I couldn't believe what I was hearing.

"In my fucking car!" he exclaimed, his voice cracking with emotion.

"What? No way!" I responded in disbelief.

He gestured toward his taxi. *"Yeah, open the door and see for yourself."*

I couldn't believe my ears. Cautiously, I approached his vehicle and opened the door. The smell hit me instantly, and then I saw it—someone had indeed shit all over the backseat. The sight was revolting. *"Someone really pu (shit) in his car,"* I thought to myself. No wonder the driver was having a nervous breakdown. This explained why he was hitting his head with both hands.

"Stop doing that," I told him firmly, referring to his self-inflicted blows. *"Did you call the police?"*

"Yes," he nodded.

"Where is the passenger now?" I asked.

"He just laughed at me and walked away," the driver explained, still visibly shaken. *"I was stunned."*

To this day, I still don't understand what kind of person could do that to someone else's taxi. Sorry, what kind of animal—though calling them an animal would be disgracing animals, since at least animals go to some corner. This was something else entirely—a person who would shit in a vehicle belonging to someone simply trying to provide transportation and take them home safely. I honestly don't know what I would do in that situation. Some lines shouldn't be crossed, and this passenger had leaped over one with reckless abandon.

Woman who left her knicker in the car

It was a busy Friday night. I'd been working non-stop since early evening and told myself, *"I'll take one more passenger and call it a night."* When a woman flagged down my taxi, I welcomed her with my usual friendly greeting. The journey passed uneventfully. Upon reaching her destination, I wished her goodnight. She smiled silently in response, merely waving her hand as she exited the vehicle. As was my habit after each customer departed, I checked the backseat for forgotten items. This time, my inspection revealed something unexpected—a red knicker lying on the floor behind the driver's seat. I was furious. How could someone leave such a private item in a stranger's taxi?

Determined to teach her a proper lesson, I reported the incident to the company. *"I'll bring the item to headquarters,"* I explained, making sure to document the discovery with time-stamped photographs as evidence. Using disposable gloves, I carefully placed the undergarment in a shoebox. The following day, I visited the company headquarters. *"As reported, I have the item in this box,"* I informed the customer service representative.

"I need to make note of the item," he replied. *"Could you open the box?"*

"I'd prefer if you opened it," I responded.

When he lifted the lid, his eyes widened in shock. *"What the hell is this?"* he demanded.

"This is the passenger's knicker," I explained calmly.

He fixed me with a stern gaze, clearly annoyed. Before he could speak, I quickly added,

"Just before you say anything—I have video recording equipment in my taxi."

I explained that after the incident, I had reviewed the footage. The recording clearly showed her removing her knicker while I was driving and deliberately tossing it onto the floor. After watching the video, the representative's demeanour changed completely.

"Don't worry," he assured me, visibly embarrassed. *"I'll teach her a good lesson."*

He wrote to inform her that she had left "a valuable personal item" in my taxi. She would need to collect it in person with valid identification. He also kept a copy of the video recording in case she caused a scene. Several days later, he called to update me.

"She came with ID," he recounted. "I gave her the box and asked her to verify the contents." Upon opening it, she erupted in anger, shouting denials and claiming to feel insulted. She threatened legal action against the company.

"Are you finished?" he had asked her coolly.

"We can prove these belong to you."

"How?" she challenged.

When he played the recording, her face reportedly turned crimson with embarrassment.

"It's illegal to record passengers in your taxi!" she protested.

"First," he countered, "it's not illegal. There are stickers on the windows clearly stating there's CCTV for driver safety. Second, if the driver didn't have this recording, you would have denied everything, which makes you a liar."

He informed her that her behaviour was completely unacceptable and closed her account.

"I'm sorry you had to deal with this," he told me afterward. "Keep up the good work."

I left wondering what could possibly motivate
someone to do something so bizarre and
inappropriate in a stranger's vehicle.

Woman is desperate to save her marriage

Being a home-based engineer, taxi driving on a part-time basis is my therapy—a means of getting out of the house and having conversations with interesting people. My line of work has endowed me with a photographic memory; faces, places, and circumstances rarely escape my mind. I picked up one night a friendly woman who greeted me warmly. As I drove away, I caught occasional glimpses in my rearview mirror. Her initial warmth had been replaced by a faraway anxious expression that showed that her mind was elsewhere. I attempted friendly conversation—my usual approach. If the passenger does not respond to these attempts, I respect the silence and endure the ride in silence. Here, though, I sensed that something disturbed her.

"Are you alright?" I whispered.

It loosened something within her. Suddenly she was crying. Tears were streaming down her cheeks.

"Are you okay, love? Do you want to talk about it?" I inquired, concerned by her distress.

She didn't know what to do, she said, her breath caught.

"Regarding what?......I'm trying to save my marriage. I'm doing all that I can, and I just cannot reach him. He has closed all the doors and won't tell me what's happening."
From my experience and age, I provided what seemed like sound advice.

"Sometimes you need one's own space so that one can break away from routines," I said.
"Give him room to breathe without withdrawing affection and love. Be gentle and not pushy. Let him approach you when he's ready and talk calmly."
We went on talking, and she seemed somewhat reassured by the end.
"I am glad that you feel better now" I said.
By the time we arrived, she'd only given the postcode and no house number—a practice she usually did for security. Something in my gut stirred, though—a sense that I hoped proved untrue.
"Is number 13 your door?" I asked.
She was visibly amazed. *"How did you know? I only gave you my postal code and not my door number so that drivers would not know exactly where I live."*
I thought fast and said, *"A guess, just my luck. Nothing else."*
She hesitated and smiled gently.
"Alright. I understand. Goodnight."

As she walked away, I knew my words were in vain. She walked into the road of heartbreak.

Two weeks earlier, I'd done a two-drop-off. First went the woman, and then the man. They were wrapped up in one another—kissing and softly giggling—promising one another things yet to come. After the good-bye kiss that involved tears, I dropped the man at his final stop: number 13. Unlike the woman this evening, he included the number on his door in the reservation information. Her husband was that man.

My "guess" wasn't luck—it was my memory connecting the pieces of a painful puzzle. As soon as I drove her home, I knew she didn't have any chance at all of saving her marriage. Her husband already had another woman. I have often wondered if I should have been honest with her. It would have hurt her horribly at the moment, but maybe it would have been more compassionate than giving her false expectations. I think that everyone deserves the unadulterated truth no matter the pain. They may hurt temporarily, yet they recover sooner than the ones who are kept in the dark and hold onto hopeless circumstances.

It is good to be good person. Happy birthday

I picked up a young girl around 3 AM after her late shift had ended. As she settled into the back seat of my taxi, I noticed her downcast expression in the rearview mirror.

"What's happening, honey?" I asked, trying to lighten the mood.

"Nothing," she replied quietly, then added, *"Do you know it's my birthday today?"*

"Really? Happy birthday!" I said with genuine enthusiasm. *"So, what are you going to do today? Any celebration planned?"*

At this question, she seemed to freeze, her face clouding with sadness.

"What's wrong?" I prompted gently.

"I don't have anyone to celebrate with," she confessed. *"Most of my family lives far away, and I have to work away from home."*

As we continued along the route, I realized we would be passing near my neighbourhood, where I knew a supermarket stayed open 24 hours. An idea began to form in my mind.

"Would you mind if I stop for a few minutes to get some water?" I asked her. *"I'm feeling a bit dehydrated."*

"OK, no problem," she answered.

I pulled up to the supermarket, where the staff knew me as a longtime local customer. I headed straight for the bakery section and, to my relief, found they had slice cakes available. I grabbed two portions and approached the cashier.

"Do you have any birthday cake candles?" I inquired.

The cashier rummaged beneath the counter. *"I might have some here,"* he said, eventually producing a small package.

"Give me two of them," I requested, *"and put the cakes and candles in a box, please."*

I also purchased some juice before finding the "Happy Birthday" song on phone app and pausing it on my phone. Then I returned to the taxi. Once inside, I pressed play on the music, lit the candles on the cakes, and presented them to my passenger. The surprise registered immediately on her face, followed by tears—happy ones this time. She turned to me with an expression of pure gratitude.

"I can't thank you enough," she said, her voice thick with emotion. *"Now I know no one is truly alone. There will always be someone out there."*

"Of course," I agreed. *"Just choose your friends wisely but never lose hope. There will always be like-minded people with good hearts out there. Just be yourself."*

She was beaming as I dropped her off at her destination. Watching her walk to her door with a spring in her step and a smile on her face filled me with satisfaction. Making this lonely young woman's birthday special, even in such a small way, reminded me why small acts of kindness matter so much. This feeling—knowing I'd brightened someone's day when they needed it most—is what keeps me going.

Oxford or Oxford Street

Another night in the middle of London. Early morning brought a job offer—a long trip. Just the thing for a quiet night; I could just complete my shift afterwards. I went to the pickup point near one of the casinos. An Indian gentleman boarded my taxi, and I asked him, as I always do, his name and where I was to drop him off. He was visibly agitated and in a terrible mood. He did not even give me a chance to get a word out before interrupting me.

"Hey, I typed in the address. Wake me up when we arrive," he snapped.

In a typical scenario, confirming addresses with customers saves us all the hassle and keeps us from making unnecessary trips. Tonight, though, he would not even allow me to get a word out, shutting me up in a rather unpleasant manner. Deep within the pit of my stomach, I sensed something was wrong with the reservation, but if he said, *"I just put the address there and wake me up when we arrive,"* it was not my business to argue with it. He already seemed to be seeking a fight.

So, I headed towards Oxford City. I drove for about an hour and a half before I arrived at the destination and woke up the passenger. That's when all hell let loose.

He looked around in confusion. *"Where the fuck am I?"*
"Wherever you put on the app," I spoke softly. He lost his temper—cursing and screaming

"That's it. I've had enough of this nonsense," I stated emphatically. *"Check your app. If I've brought you to the wrong location, I'll simply take you back free of charge. But if not, you're out of my taxi."*
"Yeah, let's take a look," he growled. The moment he glanced at his app, his face dropped, and I heard a lone word: *"Shit."*
"exactly" I said.
He did calm down a great deal afterwards. I reminded him I'd tried to explain his last drop-off location to him and that he'd rudely cut me off. I'd been going on the directions on the app, though in my mind I'd suspected him to have been referring to "Oxford Street," which would have been a maximum of a 15-minute drive. Well, tough luck. If he had let me do my job and allowed me to check, he wouldn't be in this situation. I ended the trip on the app and informed him that he would need to take a different taxi to London.
"It's 4 o'clock. How am I going to find one? Every where's as quiet as the dead," he protested.
"You'll have to pay me then. I'm not going to do it for free," I said.

Deep within him, if only he was respectful to me, we would not have been there in the first place. And even if we did, I would have provided him with a free ride. But since he was so impolite, a free ride was not possible. We bargained over the price, and I requested him to pay in advance, and so he did. On the way back to London, He rode in the front passenger seat. He never closed his eyes and began talking to me. I eventually discovered the root of his woes—he'd lost £10,000 at the casino and was looking for someone to take it out on. Unfortunately, I was the someone, but it cost him even more. During the drive back, we talked more seriously. We made a few stops to have a cup of coffee at the petrol stations. I later dropped him off at his real address—where he should have been dropped off in the first place.

"Wait patiently next time the driver is just doing his job and double checking the details," I said to him. *"You might find yourself in Scotland otherwise."*

His response surprised me.

"First of all, I am sorry for being a jerk and taking my own mistake out on you," he apologized earnestly. *"I got what I deserved and learned my lesson. Next time, I'll definitely double check my destination, verify with the driver, and be respectful to them."*

The lesson? Never take out your frustrations on someone else for your own mistakes. Karma makes you pay double and learn the hard way. Always treat the person who picks you up at 2:30 in the morning and drives you home with courtesy. They are only doing their job.

Acting to Pretend to Be a Boyfriend

I was driving to central London to start work. I stopped at the area around Highgate and picked up my very first passenger in the evening hours—a woman who was very respectful and kind to me. We conversed on the journey. She was off to a popular nightclub and disco in Camden Town. I dropped her off and wished her a nice night, her cheerful attitude having set me up for the shift. I spent the whole night working and was driving back when, going past the same nightclub, I noticed a familiar face. It was her—the woman who was so nice to me before—sitting on the ground, frantically waving her hands around like,

"Go away. leave me alone." There were two men looming over her while she appeared defenceless.

I did not hesitate. I stopped my taxi next to her and stormed out, playing the role:

"Hey, Kel!

What the heck are you doing? You are supposed to be home early!" She was surprised at my sudden arrival but quickly recognized my face and did not say a word when I turned to the two men.

"What are you staring at in the world? What are you up to?" I asked.

Their defence was the usual one:

"We're only trying to assist her."
"No need," I said. "She's, my girlfriend." I turned
to her and commanded, "Get in the car now!"

She obeyed immediately. I knew where she lived
since we made the trip previously, so I brought
her there and knocked on the door. Her
boyfriend showed up and, upon seeing her in my
taxi, stormed out, ready to fight.

*"Wait a minute, mate, hold your horse" I said,
putting up my hands. "You listen to me first. If
you still want to have a fight afterwards, fine,
we'll have a fight. But at least listen to me,
hear me out."*
I quickly explained to him that I was her driver
a short while prior. I informed him what I
observed—how she needed help, how courteous
and respectful she was to me, and how I felt I
was under an obligation to assist her at the
time. I explained how I pretended to be her
boyfriend to ward off the other men, safely
placed her in my taxi, and brought her home.

*"And if you still want to have a fight, fine," I
said.*
He was so embarrassed when I told him the
whole story. He asked me to help get her into
the house, which I did. When I was leaving, he
said,

*"One minute," and tried to hand me £40.
"What is this for?" I asked.*

41

I shook my head.

He insisted, "Have a drink on me, please. I was rather stupid when you arrived at the door. Perhaps an apology isn't sufficient, but at least have a drink on me, please." We should never assume anything until we have the whole truth. This only leads to unnecessary circumstances and embarrassment when the truth is revealed.

Stupid Drug Dealer

I confirmed a job on my screen and went to the pickup spot. A woman approached my taxi and said,

"I ordered it. I'm sending my sister something to eat." She said "she" initially, then "he."

Obviously, red flags started waving.

The taxi cost her approximately £60. She could have easily ordered from one of the online ordering websites, had it delivered to her sister's and had it paid for on her side. I did not believe her, but I could not argue with her either—a job was a job. Something did not smell right, and I knew it was illegal. I started driving slowly and, a few miles down the road, called the police on my other phone (as she could track my movement on her app) and told them what had happened and the fact that I did not want to be involved in anything illegal that I might be transporting. I was put on hold for a few seconds by the operator. She then told me,

"Someone will call on this number."

I was at least relieved now since everything was on record. A few seconds later, I was on the call. A police officer told me,

"Listen, appreciate the call and concern. We are behind you. Do not get frustrated and agitated—you have done the right thing in calling and reporting it. We were already

Wow. I was stunned. Basically, they were already monitoring this operation and following me to find the other person or people on the receiving end. They told me to stay calm and let me know they would move in once someone would show up to pick up the package. I drove for a further 15 minutes before I arrived at the destination. I sent a message to let them know I was there, and a gentleman approached my taxi slowly. Suddenly flashing blue and red lights everywhere. They arrested the man and took my statement. I was already transparent since I was the person who had made the call while I was on the move. The police officers who were chasing me approached and thanked me for being a considerate person and for being so cooperative. I constantly tell my other fellow drivers: if your passenger requests that you drop off something, ask them what it is. If you're not certain, simply call the police—you never know what is going to happen next. There are people out there using taxi firms like personal couriers for their criminal activities. I may have taken a long time explaining myself, even if I was able to establish my innocence from the company job records, If I hadn't have called the police on the way and explained the situation. Acting quickly was less hassle and the right thing to do. Or, if uncertain, just turn the job down.

Black Taxi Show Off, Face Off

I was driving down through central London when a Black Taxi driver pulled up alongside me. He lowered his window and started shouting across with a thick cockney accent.

"Hey... you! This is 20 miles an hour road, do you know it?"

The thing was, I wasn't even driving above 20 mph. He was clearly showing off to impress the woman passenger sitting in the back of his taxi. I glanced over at him and his vehicle, taking in the scene before responding.

"Before lecturing me and showing off about how and what speed I drive, put your lights on!!! It's nighttime, so-called professional driver."

I could see his woman passenger in the back start laughing uncontrollably—she was absolutely in stitches at his expense. His face fell immediately, the cockiness vanishing in an instant. I simply drove off, leaving him to deal with his embarrassment. The lesson? Before making comments about others, we should take a good look at ourselves first.

I am not getting paid to lie for you

I picked up a man and a woman for a two-drop off journey. Upon arrival at the first destination, the woman requested if I could wait for approximately 30 minutes. I replied that I receive waiting time pay, so I did not have any problem with doing this. Both of them got out together. She returned to the taxi after thirty to forty minutes. Her phone kept ringing, and every time she got a call, I could hear her apologizing for traffic congestion and roadblocks for her apparent lack of punctuality. Something did not feel right in the entire situation. Right before we arrived at the final destination, she made a peculiar request.

"If he asks, tell him there was a traffic jam and a road blockage, please."

I was upset. *"Sorry, madam,"* I answered gruffly, *"I'm here to take you wherever you wish to go, but I'm not being paid to tell lies for you. If the man approaches and asks me any questions, I'll simply tell him the truth. If you don't want that, make sure he has no chance to speak to me."*

She leapt out of the taxi, quickly pinning down the man and struggling with him. She waved wildly to me to "go"—clearly meaning me to drive away. My job is straightforward:

transport passengers from point A to point B. There are others who incorrectly believe that because they're paying, they can get whatever they want. Sorry to them, but that's not how it works. Integrity cannot be bought, not even for the price of a Taxi fare.

Life is So Strange

Another weekend, another late-night taxi journey. I picked up a young girl outside one of London's expensive hotels. Her route seemed to be heading almost toward my home, so I decided to drop her off and call it a night.

At first glance, she appeared at least 18—tall and grown. She was dressed flashily, in clothes that seemed cheap yet tried to be stylish. Her appearance raised questions in my experienced mind. Coming out of an expensive hotel at 4 AM, dressed to impress, and heading to an average neighbourhood—something didn't quite add up.

But it wasn't my place to judge or question passengers, especially those who appeared to be of legal age. She pretended to be posh, but underneath, I sensed she was just dreaming of something more extravagant in life. We exchanged minimal conversation during the short journey, and I dropped her off near my neighbourhood.

Days later, I went to my daughter's school to pick her up for a doctor's appointment. That's when life served up its most shocking twist.

The same girl from that night was there. I could hardly believe my eyes.

"Do you know her?" I asked my daughter.

"Yes, but not very closely," she replied."I don't like some of her attitudes and show-offs—always bragging about new phones, clothes, and shoes. Sometimes she asks us to hang out, but we ignore her.

"How old is she?" I inquired, already sensing something was wrong.

"She's 15," my daughter answered.

I didn't know how to respond. My mind was reeling.

Later at home, I made my daughter promise not to discuss what I was about to tell her with anyone. When she agreed, I shared everything I knew. She was shocked.

"No wonder she was always getting expensive stuff," my daughter muttered.

"That's not our place to judge," I told her. "But remember this: you can have everything in life at the right time. First, finish your education. Get good qualifications. Once you have a solid job, you can buy whatever you can afford. Just never cross a line that might bring you shame."

I emphasized the importance of walking a straight path.

"As your father, I'll always be here for you, as long as you keep yourself on the right track."

She cuddled me, thanking me and saying how lucky she was to have me as a father. The lesson is profound: it's easy to bring a child into this world and call yourself a parent. The most crucial responsibility is guiding them until they're mature enough to distinguish between right and wrong.

When a 15-year-old is wandering home at 5 AM and her parents aren't questioning or stopping her, the parents—not the child—are truly at fault. If you're responsible for bringing a life into this world, you must guide them until they understand the difference between good and bad paths. I felt deeply troubled. Some might question why I didn't report the situation. It was complicated—the booking was under an apparently mature name, making it easy for others to deny responsibility and potentially leave me in a difficult position. Moreover, her makeup and dress made her appear older than her actual age.

Life, indeed, can be startlingly strange.

Cheeky and Crafty Customer

I am often surprised at the extent to which individuals will go to obtain a free ride. This short story perfectly illustrates the creativity some passengers employ to dodge paying their fare. I picked up a passenger, and our trip quickly merged onto the highway. Experienced drivers and riders are aware of the golden rule: you cannot simply drop a person off on a highway. You must reach a place of safety, an exit, or a suitable stopping point. Most of my regular passengers know this rule. But this particular passenger had other ideas. After we had been on the highway for a while, he attempted a sly trick—cancelling the ride on his app.

Just like that.

Clearly, he was hoping for a free ride home. But I was not about to let that happen. Fortunately, an exit was just ahead. With a quick twist of the steering wheel, I veered off the highway and found the nearest petrol station.

 "You'll have to get out here," I told him firmly.

I notified the head office of the occurrence, later learning he'd attempted this trick twice before. The moment he cancelled the ride; the job was legally terminated. I could no longer transport him—nor was I legally obligated to do so. It was just another day evidencing the innovative ways some people try to get something for nothing.

This is not your personal mobile kitchen...

The evening traffic crawled, a serpentine line of headlights cutting through the city's twilight. I was midway through my shift, another routine taxi ride with a passenger who seemed oblivious to the unwritten rules of shared transit. She was a young Indian woman, perhaps in her mid-twenties, who had just settled into the back seat. At first, everything seemed ordinary—until a pungent aroma of curry began to permeate the car's interior. Glancing back, I caught her in the act: carefully spooning warm curry onto a plate, right there in my taxi.

"*Excuse me,*" I said, my tone measured but firm, "*could you please pack that up? Eating isn't permitted in the taxi.*"

Her initial response was a dismissive continuation of her meal. When I repeated my request, her reply was both shocking and entitled.

"*But I'm paying for this ride,*" she declared, her eyes meeting mine in the rear-view mirror with a defiance that bordered on arrogance.

"*Being a paying passenger doesn't make this your personal mobile kitchen,*" I retorted. "*There's a basic courtesy of asking before assuming you can do whatever you want.*"

"Yes, I am entitled," she shot back, her words hanging in the air like the lingering curry scent.

In that moment, a line has been crossed. Professionalism and respect were non-negotiable in my taxi. I pulled over,

"I instructed coldly." This journey is terminated."

The roadside became our impromptu endpoint, a testament to the fact that a financial transaction does not grant unlimited privileges. As I processed the termination and prepared to file a report, I reflected on a fundamental truth: in any service—be it transportation or otherwise—mutual respect is not just recommended, it is required.

Most common questions and things in a ride

- Every ride begins with a familiar script. The passenger slides into the back seat, and seconds later, the familiar questions start coming.
- "Do you have a charger?" The unavoidable opening line, as though the taxi is a mobile charging station. Smartphones clutched tightly, passengers turn to the front console with desperate hope, the battery indicator of their phone blinking its last warning.
- Next comes the Bluetooth ritual. Five-minute journeys mysteriously transform into complex technical negotiations. Passengers will spend the entire short ride wrestling with connection protocols, fingers dancing across smartphone screens. "Can I connect?" they will ask, even as the destination comes into view just blocks away. Connecting is a mini-drama—five precious minutes of device pairing as the city whizzes by outside the windows.
- "How long?" The question echoes, despite the ETA being clearly displayed on their ride app. It is an odd dance of redundancy, as though the journey is made more

authentic by hearing the estimated time from the driver.

- But beneath these minor annoyances lie the true tests of a driver's patience. Smoking—barred absolutely—is an ongoing offense. The mere hint of a cigarette's existence sends a shiver down any taxi spine. Some passengers seem to view the "No Smoking" sign as a mere suggestion, not a hard rule.
- Door slamming becomes an art form of disrespect. Each slam with force is like a personal insult, the body of the taxi shaking from the extra energy. It's not just a door; it's a statement of carelessness. The media player becomes a battleground. Wandering hands reach out, adjusting volumes to ear-shattering decibels or pressing buttons randomly. Each touch is a potential distraction, a moment that can disrupt the driver's concentration and, more critically, the safety of the passengers.

These are the unwritten rules of the road, the tacit understanding between driver and passenger. A contract written in patience, marked by the rhythm of city streets and the constant negotiation of public space.

I do not feel safe to drive with you

The Shoreditch night traffic crawled along, a typical London backdrop to what would otherwise have been a routine taxi ride. I'd picked up a young woman heading south, the pulse of the city pounding around us. At a red light, the unimaginable happened—a blur of motion, an open door, and a stranger sliding into the front passenger seat. My first response was subdued but direct.

"What are you doing?"

The words hung, filled with a combination of confusion and increasing tension.

"Take me home," he said, as if his presence itself was explanation enough.

This was not an appointment pickup. No notice, no agreement—just an unexpected invasion of my taxi's fiercely protected personal space. I stopped; my alarm evident: safety. Not just my own, but also that of my fare-paying passenger.

"You must leave," I told him, my tone not allowing any discussion.

The argument erupted. I turned to the woman, seeking clarification.

"Do you know this man?"

Her response—or lack thereof—spoke volumes. I strode around to the front passenger side with calculated deliberation. One quick movement, and the intruder was out of the taxi. The door shut with a solid click. What happened next was incredible. The woman—the very one I was defending—began to criticize me.

"You were too harsh," she said, her comment a stunning response to a potential threat.

The universe conspired when a police car pulled up, catching the tail of our fight. The officer listened, judged, and delivered a verdict that validated my actions.

"He was protecting both of you,"

He told her, his words a bureaucratic stamp of approval on my instincts. But the damage was already there. Trust had been lost.

"Under the safety act," I said, my voice steady, *"I no longer feel safe to continue this trip. I cannot transport a passenger who fails to understand the fundamental principles of personal security."*

The journey came to an end. Not with a bang, but with a profound realization about the uncertainty of human nature. There are some, I imagined, who would fight protection even when it is offered freely and without hesitation.

Thank you darling

The city slumbered, but Acton's streets still buzzed with the muted liveliness of a weekend night. It was past two in the morning when I arrived to pick her up, the taxi a refuge of warmth from the chill of late-night London. We chatted easily at first, but tension crept in as she shared her concern.

"There are two men," she said, her voice tight with fear. *"They've been lurking around my doorstep. I don't feel safe."*

Her vulnerability touched a chord.

"Listen," I said, *"if that's what's happening, I'll walk you to your door. I'll be your pretend boyfriend. They won't bother you again."*

Surprise twirled in her eyes.

"Really? You'd do that for me?"

"Of course," I assured her. *"I know how frustrating and scary it can be to live alone."*

When we approached her street, the men were there—just as she'd described. I parked carefully, locked the taxi, and walked her to her door in deliberate strides. When she unlocked the door, I made sure to speak loudly.

"I'll get some things from the shop. Do you want anything, darling?"

My gaze locked on the pair of men, a silent challenge.

"Are you lost, mates?"

The question hung in the air, thick with unspoken threats.

"No, just walking around," they mumbled.

"This is our doorstep," I stated resolutely. "If you don't have business here, I'd advise you to move on."

Her response was immediate.

"No, thank you, darling. Nothing needed."

I called out loud, saying,

"I'll return as soon as possible," so that they could hear each word. Days went by, and then there was a message. "Those men did not return. After you walked me to my door," she wrote, "and made the scene you did, they never bothered me again. I don't know how to thank you."

Sometimes late at night, assistance comes in unexpected forms—a taxi driver, a flash of solidarity, a shield against potential harm.

Endless Trip

The nightscape of London was a blur through the taxi windows—a kaleidoscope of streetlights and dark corners. What had begun as a straightforward trip was soon dissolved into a marathon of confusion and misinformation. The passenger was drunk; that was clear from the moment he fell into the back seat. His coordination seemed as scrambled as his intended address. Each arrival was met with the same bewildered response:

.*"This isn't my address."*

Thirty minutes here, forty minutes there—the meter running, patience wearing thin. I'd point to his own app, the digital evidence of him continually changing destinations.

"Look, mate, this is what you typed; are you sure?" I said.

"Sorry, I made a mistake," he would say, and type in a different address.

The third occasion he claimed familiarity with some undisclosed location, irritation bubbled just beneath a surface of professional poise.

"Do you actually know where you're going?" The question lingered, heavy with unspoken exasperation.

"Yeah, I know," he insisted unconvincingly.

After about 3 hours detouring around with his permission—and recognizing his impaired state—I scrolled through his contacts and found his wife's number. A quick phone call revealed the truth: his home was only ten minutes from our original pickup point, but we have been driving around from one point to another almost last 3 hours. By the time we arrived, she was waiting. She was not upset about the roundabout route or his intoxication but something far more complicated.

"You've been taking him to his ex-girlfriends houses," she accused, her voice a thunderclap of revelation.

I did not need any part in their domestic drama. *"Please, just get him out,"* I begged, wanting to escape the brewing storm.

As they disappeared into their home, I reflected on the night's unscheduled detour. Some journeys, I mused, are about more than miles travelled.

Do you want to drive, sweetheart?

Heathrow Airport buzzed with the typical chaos of international arrivals. I had been reserved for a meet-and-greet, standing poised to collect a passenger fresh from the States. As she walked towards me, dragging her luggage, I gestured towards the taxi.

"The car's open," I yelled. "Just get in yourself. I'll be back in a minute when I pay the parking charge."

Minutes later, ticket in hand, I returned to a scene that would be another chapter in my taxi adventure book. There she was, sitting comfortably—on the driver's side. I got in quietly, sliding into the front passenger seat and shutting the door. Her confused eyes met mine.

"Can we go?" she said.

A smile played at the edges of my mouth.

"Sure, sweetheart. Here are the keys. Want to drive?"

"What do you mean?"

"Well, you're sitting in the driver's seat—at least, in England," I explained, barely containing my amusement.

Her epiphany was comically instantaneous.

"Shit. Oh my god, I knew something was weird. Why is this wheel here?"

We both burst out laughing. The universal language of confusion bridged our temporary cultural divide. We both got out and switch the places. The mix-up was an old one—a testament to the subtle differences that can catch even seasoned travellers off guard. Certain trips, I have found, start many miles before the initial mile is travelled.

No Way

The gentle Sunday morning sunlight filtered through the windows of the taxi, bringing a warm glow to three American tourists. Their voices hummed in the background, the typical morning chatter of sightseers seeing London. Then something clicked—One of the passenger voice that tugged at the edges of memory.

"Is your name Kevin?" The words escaped before I could stop them.

There was a sudden, heavy silence.

"Yes," came the reply. "How do you know my name?"

I pulled the taxi over to the side of the road, activating the hazard lights. I turned around, facing the passenger.

"It's me, Kevin."

"No way," he whispered.

Years melted away in that instant. We were once friends when I was in the States—when talking to each other was not as simple as a quick message. When I returned to London, we had lost touch, our connection severed by distance and time. And there he was now, by some quirk of destiny, sitting in my taxi. Learning they were leaving at noon; I asked them out on a farewell tour of London—my treat. I thought they might be hungry, so I took them to a 24-hour cafe, where I bought them a decent breakfast. By 10 am, we had collected their bags from the hotel to drop them off and were headed to the airport. The world, I figured, is a lot smaller than we imagine. All those years of searching long lost friend, and there he was—a passenger in my taxi in London. We are friends to this day, a friendship rekindled by the most improbable of journeys.

Best ever, never friends

The evening began innocently enough. Four young women, squeezed into my taxi, their laughter filling the small space. Each drop-off seemed to initiate some odd ritual—a burst of whispers that unfolded like a well-practiced act. As the first passenger left, the trio's discussion changed. Smiles that had just seconds before seemed friendly now turned into razor-edged remark. The missing friend was their victim, her personality torn apart with an offhand viciousness that gave the lie to their previous friendship. With each passenger dropped off, the cycle repeated itself. They dropped one by one to the group's collective disapproval. Their friendship seemed a fragile thing—built on in-person laughter, dismantled in whispers the moment backs were turned. The final passenger, alone now, completed the ritual. She phoned one of her friend and illustrated the final betrayal.

"I simply didn't want to go out with them, darling," she confessed to an unseen friend, her voice dripping with contempt.

From my position behind the steering wheel, I witnessed a human drama that didn't add up. These weren't friends, after all, but actors in an elaborate charade of closeness. Some bonds, I discovered, are as disposable as they are devastating—a chain of gossip more binding than any genuine friendship.

Gold digger of all time

Knightsbridge glimmered in the evening light, its exclusive restaurants a backdrop to countless romantic encounters. I'd just collected a young woman who moments ago had shared an affectionate farewell with an attractive gentleman outside one of the area's most prestigious establishments. One conversations are never meant to be overheard. But in the confined space of a taxi, secrets have a way of escaping.

Her phone call to her mother began innocently enough.

"Mum, I think this time I hit the jackpot," she said, her voice bubbling with excitement.

The phone, carelessly set to speaker, broadcast her true intentions with crystal clarity. Her mother's response was equally calculated. *"Keep him happy,"* she advised, her tone a mixture of coaching and conspiracy. The conversation unfolded like a carefully orchestrated plan. A potential wedding gift of a million pounds, a startup funding waiting in the wings—these were not tokens of love, but calculated investments. The daughter's strategy was laid bare: maintain an illusion of affection, keep him "warm and exciting," all while eyeing the financial prize.

"Don't scare him," her mother cautioned. "Let him give you everything."

I remained silent, a reluctant witness to a romance built not on genuine emotion, but on financial calculation. The gentleman—presumably in love, believing in the authenticity of their connection—was unknowingly part of an elaborate performance. As we travelled through London's streets, I couldn't help but feel a profound sadness. Love, in this moment, had been reduced to a transaction.

I did everything for you

The London streets hosted numerous dramas, yet none were as wild and untamed as the one unfolding in my taxi. An African woman, her voice a mix of desperation and anger, clutched her phone like an emotional war tool.

"What did she have that I didn't?" The question hung in the air, heavy with wounded pride and increasing anger.

Her monologue painted such a clear picture of devotion—middle-of-the-night taxi rides fuelled by desire, indulging every whim, being "24/7" available. Each word was an elegy to a relationship that was on the verge of destruction.

"I did everything for you," she repeated, her voice a crescendo of betrayal.

We arrived at the destination—a nondescript building that would be the backdrop for her final showdown. She burst from the taxi, a physical declaration of defiance. Spinning, gesturing, daring—she demanded answers from an unseen foe.

"What did you find on her?"

The words echoed off the building's walls. Her boyfriend eventually relented, tossing her keys out of a window. A rushed transfer of funds followed, bringing a close to their tumultuous connection. On the ride home, her voice continued—a steady soundscape of pain and anger. I remained silent, a stoic observer of human complexity. Some journeys, I've found, cover more emotional miles than physical miles.

Ohh... My baby

The tension was palpable the moment they entered my taxi. A couple, separated by an invisible wall of silence, with the baby seated between them like a buffer. Their bodies spoke volumes—turned away from each other, communicating through obstinate silence. Twenty minutes of complete silence passed. When we reached their destination, they robotically opened their doors and exited, walking towards their house with mechanical precision. It was not until they were midway to their door that I noticed something profoundly wrong. The baby remained.

"*Sorry, ma'am,*" I yelled, my voice cutting through the night, "*I have children of my own. I don't have to adopt yours.*"
The break of understanding was instantaneous. The woman spun around, horror etching her face.

"*Oh, my baby!*"
She hurried back, snatching the child from the baby chair. Suddenly, their earlier quarrel was forgotten. Sweet words and gentle caresses replaced the earlier chilly silence—as if they had never had a fight. I was left wondering: How could two people who had a child's life in their hands be so disconnected that they could simply walk away, leaving behind their most

precious asset? Some journeys reveal more about man than about the miles travelled.

Let's party...

The week had been a marathon of monotony, each mile driven feeling heavier than the last. Two boys and two girls entered my taxi, their energy a stark contrast to my weary disposition. What began as a routine journey quickly transformed into something unexpected. Laughter filled the taxi—jokes traded; stories shared. By the time we reached their destination, a vibrant nightclub, something had shifted. They turned to me, their invitation genuine and warm.

"Why don't you join us? Life's too short."

I initially declined, professional duty weighing on my shoulders. But something stirred inside—a desire to break free from the routine, to breathe life into a tired spirit. As they walked towards the club, I surprised even myself. A quick beep of the horn, a lowered window.

"Do you still want me to come?"

"Yes!" came the unanimous response.

One minute to park. A quick decision to step out of my professional persona.

"Let's party tonight," I declared.

The night unfolded in a whirlwind of music, laughter, and unexpected companionship. They insisted on buying the drinks, refusing my offers to pay. I remained the responsible one—no alcohol, ready to drive—but the joy was intoxicating enough. When the night concluded, I dropped them home, feeling renewed. Sometimes, spontaneity is the best antidote to life's monotony.

Take me 15 Pounds worth distance please

The city slumbered; the streets illuminated by occasional streetlights as I accepted the dispatch. A central London pickup—a minute's distance. The scene developed with a familiarity that stirred paternal instincts. She was young—barely eighteen, with an outfit that screamed inexperience and a desperate desire to belong. The boy's goodbye was casual, almost dismissive. He watched her get into the taxi without concern for her safety, without offering to walk her home.

"Is he your boyfriend?"
I asked, my tone neutral but with a tinge of unspoken concern.

"Yes,"
She replied, her voice a mix of youth and uncertainty. The evening wore on, and then, diffidently, her request. Fifty pounds was beyond her means. "Could you take me fifteen pounds worth of distance?" There was no missing the vulnerability in her voice. I'd seen so many passengers, but there was something about her that reminded me of my own daughter. The arithmetic of the moment dissolved into something more profound.

"How much do you have?" I asked.
"Fifteen pounds," she answered.

I responded at once.

"I'll take ten for petrol," I told her, "And you can keep the remainder for yourself. I'll get you home safely."

Her surprise was palpable.

"Are you sure?"

"It's not all about money," I said. "Doing good sometimes generates currency of its own. Karma finds its own ways of reciprocating kindness." And " Also, some people lie and they run away to avoid fare, but you were honest and told me in advance that, So this the reward for your honesty " I said.

I gave more than a ride that night—I gave direction. Fatherly advice on choosing friends, on knowing the difference between temporary excitement and genuine concern. She listened, genuinely grateful.

www.ingramcontent.com/pod-product-compliance
Lightning Source LLC
Chambersburg PA
CBHW040623020826
48978CB00013BD/1248